D0817430

BROWN COW

Originally printed by Doubleday and Company.
Library of Congress Control Number: 2003103726

ISBN: 978-0-89272-602-8

FARM

A COUNTING BOOK
BY DAHLOV IPCAR

Down East

It is wintertime on Brown Cow Farm. The animals are all inside the big brown barn. Outside, the barnyard is piled high with cold white snow. There is snow on the barn roof too, and long shiny icicles hang from the eaves. High up on the roof top is a weather-vane cow showing that the cold north wind is blowing, but inside the big barn, where the animals are, it is snug and warm.

There is one brown horse in a big box stall. A big shiny brown horse with a
long black tail and a wavy black mane. Farmer Brown feeds her oats and hay
and brushes her and combs her mane.

There are two brown hound dogs that sleep in the hay. Two brown hound dogs with long brown ears. They wag their tails and sniff the air.

2

3 There are three brown cats that live in the barn. They drink white milk and catch brown rats and sleep in the hayloft up under the eaves.

There are four brown rabbits in a rabbit hutch. They have long ears and soft brown fur. They wiggle their noses and hop about, and they nibble on carrots and cabbages and hay.

4

5 There are five fat brown pigs in a smelly pig pen. They snortle and snuffle and grunt and eat. They eat and eat lots of corn, and they root in the deep straw with their noses.

There are six brown geese with long necks, knobs on their beaks, and big web feet. They hiss and honk and bow their heads.

6

There are seven brown ducks that squabble and quack, and dabble and splash in the water pan.

7

8 There are eight brown turkeys with big fantails.

There are nine brown hens with zigzag combs.

9

10 And there are ten brown cows on Brown Cow Farm. Ten brown cows with curly horns, and tails with tassels at the ends.

They stand in their stalls and they all give milk.
Farmer Brown milks them twice each day.

When springtime comes to Brown Cow Farm the air is warm and the pastures green. The apple trees are all in bloom. High above in the windy sky, ten wild geese fly home to nest in the marshlands.

And once again all the farm animals can run about outside in the warm sunshine and eat the new green grass.

And in the springtime the baby animals
are born.

The big brown horse has one brown colt. A little brown colt with long wobbly legs, a shaggy short mane, and a black bottle-brush tail.

The ten brown cows each have a little brown calf. And that makes ten little brown calves. Ten little brown calves that play all day in the green meadows where their mothers are grazing.

10

Each of the two brown hound dogs has ten puppies. And that makes twenty fat little puppies.

one

two

three

four

five

six

seven

eight

nine

ten

20

eleven

twelve

thirteen

fourteen

fifteen

sixteen

seventeen

eighteen

nineteen

twenty

Twenty little puppies with little short legs, waggly tails, and short floppy ears.

30

The three brown cats each have ten little kittens.

And that makes thirty kittens. Thirty little soft furry kittens, purring or sleeping or playing with each other's tails.

The four brown rabbits have baby rabbits too. Each one has ten baby bunnies.

40

So there are forty brown baby bunnies hopping about and eating green leaves just as their mothers do.

50 The five fat brown pigs each have ten little piglets.

And that makes fifty baby piglets, squeaking and squealing and playing in the dirt, or sleeping alongside their big fat mothers.

The six brown geese sit on eggs in their nests until they hatch out their baby goslings. Each goose hatches ten little goslings.

60

All together there are sixty baby goslings that follow behind the mother geese.

The seven brown ducks each hatch ten baby ducklings. So there are seventy little baby ducklings that swim in the duck pond and dive and splash with their mothers.

70

The eight brown turkeys hatch out eighty baby turkey poults. Each big mother turkey has ten baby poults, and she shows them how to catch little bugs to eat.

80

90

The nine brown hens hatch out ninety baby chicks. The mother hens scratch in the dirt for worms. Each mother hen has ten little chicks that peep and peck and try to scratch too.

And out in the marshes the ten wild geese build their nests and lay their eggs and hatch their babies. Each wild mother goose hatches ten little goslings.

100

That's a lot of little wild goslings. One hundred goslings that swim with their
mothers and hide in the tall grass of the wild marshlands.

There are chickens, kittens, a colt, and ducklings. Turkey poults and baby goslings. Puppies, bunnies, piglets, and calves.

And all of their big mothers too. There are lots of animals on Brown Cow Farm. Can you count them all?